JANE HISSEY

Old Bear

BIRTHDAY BOOK

JANE HISSEY
Old Bear
BIRTHDAY BOOK

BARRON'S
NEW YORK

First edition for the United States published in 1990
by Barrons Educational Series Inc.
Reprinted 1991

First published in Great Britain in 1990 by
Ebury Press Stationery
an imprint of the Random Century Group
Random Century House, 20 Vauxhall Bridge Road,
London SW1V 2SA

Reprinted in 1991

All enquiries should be addressed to:
Barron's Educational Series, Inc.
250 Wireless Boulevard
Hauppauge, New York 11788

International Standard Book No. 0-8120-6154-3

Printed in Singapore

This book belongs to

Name

Address

Introduction

When children are playing, a year between birthdays seems too long. They give their toys lots of birthdays every year – sometimes as many as one a week! Perhaps that is why some toys age faster than others. Those are the ones that are played with the most and therefore accumulate the greatest number of birthdays.

Nearly all the toys in my drawings live with us. They are part of the family. Old Bear has been with me since my first birthday, many of the others "arrived" when my children were born. The toys grow older too; they lose their hair, sag a little in the middle, have trouble with their joints, their eyes and their ears. But, just like some of their human companions, they become more lovable and more full of character and interest as the years go by. Each has a story to tell (or would have if it were not a secret).

This little book will help you to remember the birthdays of family and friends. I hope it will be with you for many years and become an old friend too.

Jane Hissey

January

1	4
2	5
3	6

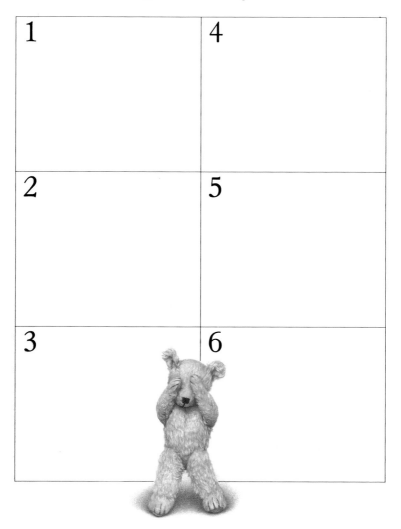

January

7	10
8	11
9	12

January

13	16
14	17
15	18

January

19	22
20	23
21	24

January

25	28
26	29
27	30

January-February

31	3
1	4
2	5

February

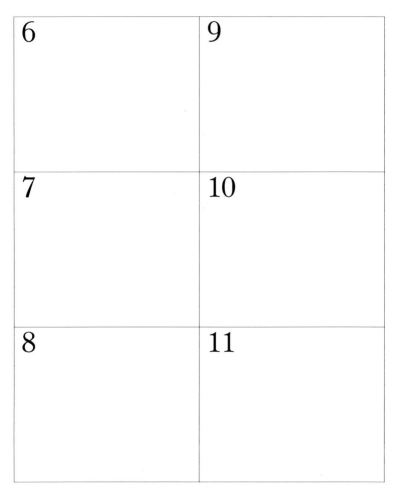

6	9
7	10
8	11

February

12	15
13	16
14	17

February

18	21
19	22
20	23

February

24	27
25	28
26	29

March

March

7	10
8	11
9	12

March

13

16

14

17

15

18

March

19	22
20	23
21	24

March

25	28
26	29
27	30

March-April

31	3
1	4
2	5

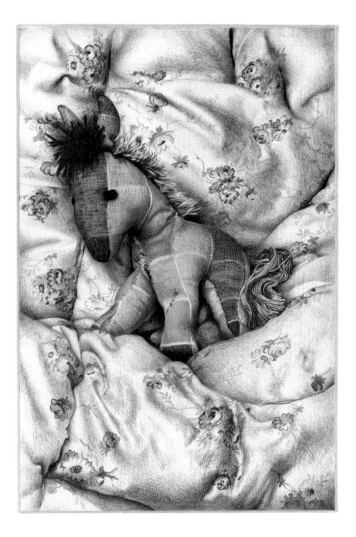

April

6	9
7	10
8	11

April

12	15
13	16
14	17

April

18	21
19	22
20	23

Jane Hissey

April

24	27
25	28
26	29

April-May

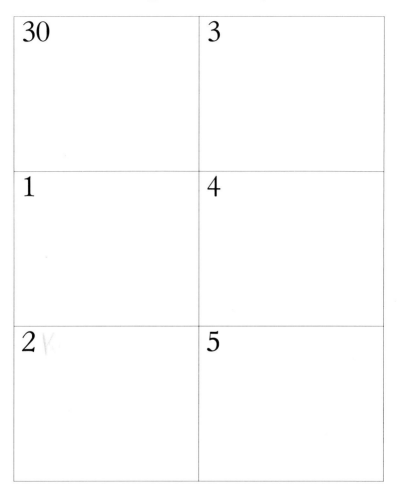

30	3
1	4
2	5

May

6	9
7	10
8 Karen's	11

May

12	15
13	16
14	17

May

18	21 *Mrs. Justin*
19	22
20	23

May

24	27
25	28
26	29

May-June

30	2
31	3
1	4

June

5	8
6	9
7	10

June

11	14
12	15
13	16

June

17	20
18	21
19	22

June

23	26
24	27
25	28

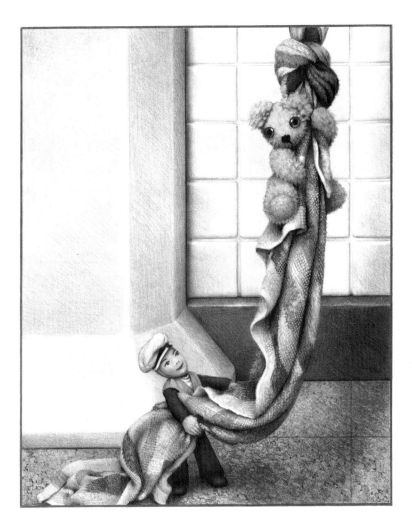

June-July

29	2
30	3
1	4

July

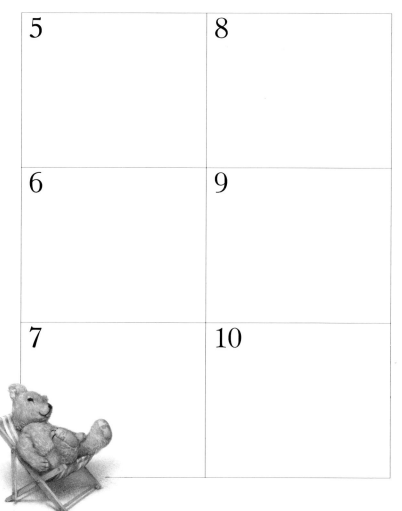

5

8

6

9

7

10

July

11	14
12	15
13	16

July

17	20
18	21
19	22

July

23	26
24	27
25	28

July-August

29	1
30	2
31	3

August

4	7
5	8
6	9

August

10	13
11	14
12	15

August

16	19
17	20
18	21

August

22	25
23	26
24	27

August-September

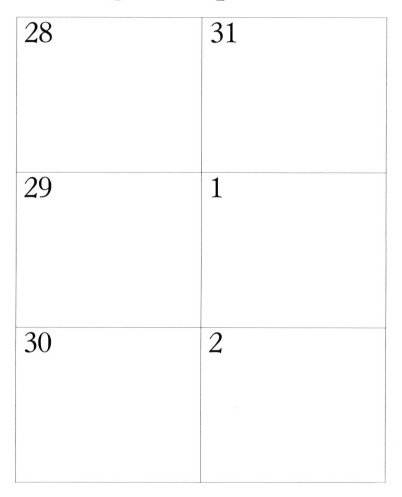

28	31
29	1
30	2

September

3	6
4	7
5	8

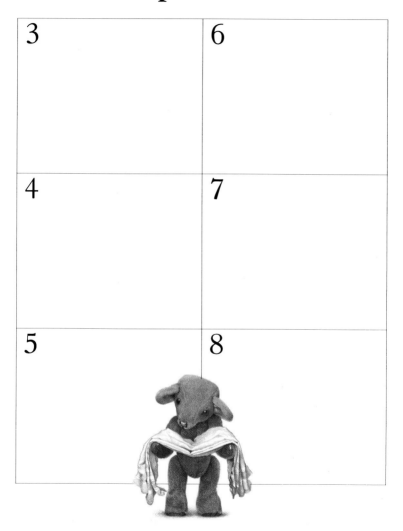

September

9	12
10	13
11	14

Blackberry & Apple

September

15	18
16	19
17	20

September

21	24
22	25
23	26

September-October

27	30
28	1
29	2

October

3	6
4	7
5	8

October

9	12
10	13
11	14

October

15

18

16

19

17

20

October

21	24
22	25
23	26

October-November

27	30
28	31
29	1

November

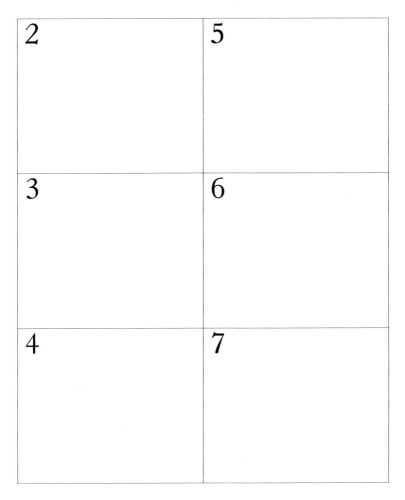

2	5
3	6
4	7

November

8	11
9	12
10 	13

November

14	17
15	18
16	19

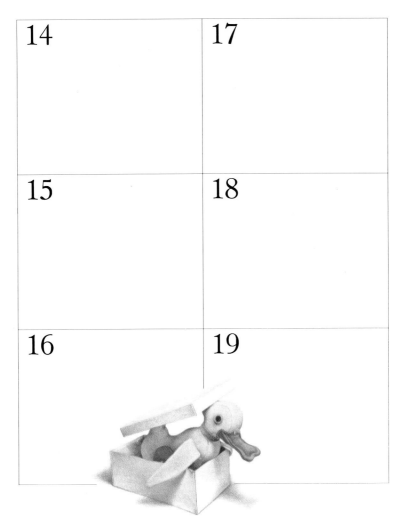

November

20	23
21	24
22	25

November-December

26	29
27	30
28	1

December

2	5
3	6
4	7

December

8	11
9	12
10	13

December

14	17
15	18
16	19

December

20	23
21	24
22	25

December

26	29
27	30
28	31